Matt the African Meerkat and Friends

Short Stories, Fuzzy Animals, and Life Lessons

Karma for Kids Books

Norma MacDonald

Matt the African Meerkat and Friends
Short Stories, Fuzzy Animals, and Life Lessons

Copyright © 2016 Norma MacDonald

First Edition

Published by: Find Your Way Publishing, Inc.
PO BOX 667
Norway, ME 04268 U.S.A.
www.findyourwaypublishing.com

ISBN-13: 978-1-945290-06-0

ISBN-10: 1-945290-06-4

Library of Congress Control Number: 2016948080

Printed in the United States of America.

Dedication

This book is dedicated to all the people trying to make the world a better place. You are making a positive difference!

"I try to live with the idea that karma is a very real thing. So, I put out what I want to get back." ~ Megan Fox

"Karma, ahhh. We sow what we reap... We reap what we sow! We reap what we sow. The law of cause and effect. And we are all under this law." ~ Nina Hagen

Table of Contents

About This Book

Welcome to our Karma for Kids Books Series. We are very grateful that you picked up this book. We believe together we can make a positive difference, one child at a time. We strive to instill important life lessons in the lives of young children. We are firm believers in Karma and think that if this simple Law of the Universe is taught to children at a young age, their lives will have the potential to be absolutely amazing.

We once knew a dog named Karma. She was a beautiful, yellow Labrador retriever. It wasn't until after she passed, at 11 years old (God bless her loyal soul.), that we realized just how fitting her name really was.

Karma is indeed a retriever.

Whatever we threw out, Karma was always happy to bring it back to us. It didn't matter what it was, she always brought it back. If we threw out garbage, she'd bring it back without question. If we threw out the most beautiful dog toy, she'd bring it back. It's the same in life. Whatever you send out, is what you will get back. Guaranteed. Every time. Our Karma for Kids Book Series hopes to instill this easy-to-understand Law of the Universe into the lives of children at a young age. The Universe wants to happily bring you all that your heart desires, and it will, effortlessly. But first, you've got to throw out what you want it to bring back to you so that it can! Have fun with this and watch the magic happen. God bless!

Find all of Norma MacDonald's Karma for Kids Books at Amazon.com.

For more of our Karma for Kids books please visit us at:

www.karmaforkidsbooks.wordpress.com
or
www.findyourwaypublishing.com

Other books that we recommend to help children succeed in all areas of their lives:

Can Camels Dance? Short Stories, Fuzzy Animals, and Life Lessons by Norma MacDonald

Arctic Adventures: Short Stories, Fuzzy Animals, and Life Lessons by Norma MacDonald

Kyle Kitten and Friends: Short Stories, Fuzzy Animals, and Life Lessons by Norma MacDonald

The Panda Family Relies on Each Other: Short Stories, Fuzzy Animals, and Life Lessons by Norma MacDonald

Pedro the Amazon Rainforest Parrot and Friends: Short Stories, Fuzzy Animals, and Life Lessons by Norma MacDonald

Kimmie Koala and Friends: Short Stories, Fuzzy Animals, and Life Lessons by Norma MacDonald

Cranky Crocodile Saves the Day: Short Stories, Fuzzy Animals, and Life Lessons by Norma MacDonald

The Many Adventures of Peppy the Emperor Penguin: Short Stories, Fuzzy Animals, and Life Lessons by Norma MacDonald

Lucy Llama and Friends: Short Stories, Fuzzy Animals, and Life Lessons by Norma MacDonald

Ethan Eagle and Friends: Short Stories, Fuzzy Animals, and Life Lessons by Norma MacDonald

Billy Brown Bear and Friends: Short Stories, Fuzzy Animals, and Life Lessons by Norma MacDonald

Humble Heron and Friends: Short Stories, Fuzzy Animals, and Life Lessons by Norma MacDonald

Peter Penguin and Friends: Short Stories, Fuzzy Animals and Life Lessons by Norma MacDonald

Alexei the Siberian Tiger and Friends at the Circus: Short Stories, Fuzzy Animals, and Life Lessons by Norma MacDonald

Guaranteed Success for Kindergarten; 50 Easy Things You Can Do Today! by Marrae Kimball

Guaranteed Success for Grade School; 50 Easy Things You Can Do Today! by Marrae Kimball

The Secret Combination to Middle School: Real Advice from Real Kids, Ideas for Success, and Much More! by Marrae Kimball

High School Success: How to Create Your Own Path, Beat Anxiety and Depression, Master Your Goals and Dreams by Marrae Kimball

Would you please consider leaving a short review for our books, online, because they help us spread the message! Children deserve the very best that life has to offer. Reviews don't have to be long, a few sentences will do, and they help more than you know! Thank you!

Matt the African Meerkat and Friends

Short Stories, Fuzzy Animals, and Life Lessons

Karma for Kids Books

Norma MacDonald

Chapter One

Masego (Blessing)

Sand shifts back and forth as hot air moves through the desert. The wind blows across the delta, too. A delta is a place where rivers flow and leave sand and rock. This special delta is in the Kalahari Desert in Africa. It has heaps and heaps of plants—ivory palms, wild figs, ebony trees and sausage trees, tall buffalo grass, water lilies and beautiful magenta flowers. The trees and plants come in all different shapes and colors. When it gets really, really hot, the many animals find a cool spot in the shade of the tall mopane forests. Fluffy mopane trees make a nice shady spot to rest in.

Animals love the delta. Hippos, elephants, and buffalo hang out together, splashing in the refreshing water. All different kinds of antelope and loads of other animals come to the water to drink. But they always have to keep an eye out for the animals that might try to eat them—lions, leopards, hyenas, and wild dogs. Up above in the skies, vultures spiral around watching everything going on below. Vultures are always on the lookout for their next meal.

The vultures aren't the only birds. Fishing owls go fishing at night. During the day the grassy areas around the delta waters are flooded with geese, herons, ibis, and storks. They watch carefully as zebras and giraffes stand side by side quenching their thirst with refreshing water.

Around the delta, if one looks carefully, one can find a mob of the cutest of the desert animals. Meerkats. Have you ever seen a meerkat? They look more like ferrets than cats. They have cute little round faces, tiny little ears, big brown eyes, and skinny tales. Meerkats like to hang out together and sit up on their hind legs, tall as small trees. But they always have to be on the lookout for danger-- dangers from the sky and dangers from the desert. So every day one of them gets asked to be on guard duty. It's a special privilege and all the young meerkats are eager to take on the job. But it's also a very important job because the lives of the entire clan are at stake.

One day, as the hot sun burned overhead, the oldest meerkat of the clan called six of the young meerkats together and told them they had passed their training and could officially guard the colony.

These six meerkats have Setswana names. Setswana is the language spoken in Botswana, the country where the Kalahari Desert is.

Masego is the oldest of the young meerkats. His name means "blessing". Then there's Mattho. His name means "eyes". Next, is Morapedi—the one who prays. And Mokgosi which means "loud cry for help". And Mothusi which means "helper". And last but not least is Malebogo — "thanks".

Masego is the first one to have his chance as guard of the clan. Before he starts, he makes sure to fill his belly with heaps of yummy food. Meerkats like to eat lots of different kinds of food. Masego's tummy rumbles, so he scoots over to a dead tree where he's sure he will find a lizard or two. Lizards are his favorite treat. Crunchy on the outside. Soft and chewy in the middle. Yum!

He hit the jackpot and was just finishing his fourth lizard when he heard the alarm. Danger from the air. All the meerkats scurried to their den and waited until the danger had passed. Whoever was on guard duty had done their job. Now it was time for Masego to take over and perform his first assignment ever.

As he walked to the special spot on the hill, many of the clan congratulated him. But they also gave him lots of advice. Many of them knew that Masego was a dreamer. They wanted to be sure he was ready for the big responsibility.

"Keep your eyes wide open."

"Don't forget to look up."

"Use your ears."

Masego nodded and smiled. He was confident that he would be able to follow their advice. His uncle had trained him very well. He knew what kind of dangers to watch for.

As he walked by a litter of three pups who were just a month old, he felt deep in his heart the importance of his new job. He had to protect the clan, and especially the little ones, from the many predators who lurked in the vast desert. Eagles, jackals, and cobras posed the biggest danger to meerkats. He just had to make sure to pay close attention.

Despite his determination, Masego had a serious weakness. Masego the Meerkat was a big daydreamer. He often got lost in his own thoughts and dreams. He could spend hours and hours staring at the horizon, wondering what could be found beyond the delta. Or at night he would sneak out of the warren and stare up at the vast starry sky and wonder what was out there. Was there a planet of meerkats out in the universe somewhere staring down at him?

Yes, Masego had a big imagination. And that wild imagination could get him in great big trouble sometimes. Sometimes his head was so far up in the clouds that he bumped into things or fell into holes. And that's exactly what happened on his way to his first guard duty.

Some of the littlest meerkats in the clan had heaps of fun digging deep, deep holes. A dozen of them had spent the entire morning digging all over the delta. The adult meerkats told them that they always needed to cover the holes when they were done, but little meerkats weren't very good listeners. And they were not very obedient, either.

Masego, eager to start his first guard duty, was imagining all the big dangers he was going to save the clan from. He imagined a giant eagle swooping down from above. As he quietly practiced the special trill that warned the others that there was danger in the sky, it happened. One second he was walking along, the next second he fell headfirst into a giant hole. And then he made a big mistake.

Without thinking, Masego accidentally trilled that special eagle warning at the top of his lungs. He hoped someone would hear his cry and come to his rescue. But he was wrong. When the meerkat clan heard that special cry they all ran as fast as they could to their underground homes!

It took Masego about five seconds to realize his mistake. But it was too late. Everyone had disappeared and there was no one to help him get out of the hole. How many times had his uncle told him he needed to stay focused? And yet he'd let his imagination get the better of him again.

After quite some time, Masego heard someone give the signal that let everyone know it was safe to come out. So, he started chirping like crazy to get the clan's attention. A few minutes later, a group of the little ones showed up and peered down at him from the edge of the hole. "What are you doing down there, Masego? Aren't you supposed to be on guard duty?" asked one of the little ones.

Masego grunted. "And aren't you little ones supposed to cover your holes when you're done digging?" he asked. "Now how about you stop staring and help me out of here."

When he'd made it out of the hole, he went to talk to his favorite uncle and he explained what happened.

"Were you daydreaming again, Masego?" his uncle asked.

Masego dropped his chin down.

Uncle put a paw across Masego's back. "I know someday you'll make a wonderful guard and blessing to the clan, my son. But you've got to learn to focus, focus, focus!"

"Thank you, Uncle."

From that day forward, Masego did his best to keep his head out of the clouds and to pay attention to what was happening around him.

Chapter Two

Mathlo (Eyes)

Mathlo the Meerkat had very good eyes. His friends called him Matt for short. Matt could spot danger from far away. Some said he was the best guard in the whole clan. Therefore, he was given a lot of guard duties. He never fell asleep on duty. He never left his post. He was an excellent guard.

Every day he ran in circles around the delta to make sure his body was in good shape. He loved to eat centipedes and millipedes and any other insects he could find. But he always made sure not to eat too much before he went on duty so that he wouldn't get sleepy. Full bellies can make one very sleepy.

Matt didn't talk much. He found that he was better able to concentrate if others didn't distract him with chatting. Some thought he was rude. But he just wanted to do a good job. Lives were at stake. He didn't have time to talk when he was busy protecting the others.

As he walked to the guard post, a couple of mothers with their group of little ones greeted him. "You're taking over the guard duty? Wonderful. We can rest easy this afternoon."

Matt made sure he always arrived early for his duty. That's what his father had taught him; to always be on time. It's better to be a half an hour early than one minute late. He didn't like to wait for people, and he didn't like to make people wait for him, either. He hurried to the hill to relieve his cousin, who'd been on duty for several hours already.

The two of them stood back to back and gazed out across the delta. Everything seemed calm. A group of elephants splashed and bathed in the river. In the distance, a giraffe family moved slowly toward the water. The afternoon sun blazed overhead and many of the animals had sought a bit of shade in the grove of trees on the other side of the river. A gentle breeze blew and rustled the leaves.

Matt's keen eyes scanned the area. All was well. "You can go now," he said to the guard he was replacing. "I've got things covered."

For the first hour, not much happened. A flock of bright pink flamingos made a big fuss as they landed in the water. But Matt didn't let them distract him from his duty. He scanned the horizon for danger. Wait! What did he see? Was that an eagle? Matt narrowed his eyes. It was big and black and coming towards them. He barked out the special warning at the top of his lungs. Matt and all the meerkats scurried down into the safety of the burrow.

But the big black thing flying through the sky was not an eagle. In fact, it wasn't a bird at all. It was an airplane! Matt and the meerkats didn't know about airplanes. They thought airplanes were big dangerous birds. And big birds were one of the meerkats biggest enemies. Sometimes things weren't what they appeared to be. Still, the meerkats had to be extra careful. Better safe than sorry.

The rest of the afternoon passed by without any incidents. Matt peered at the sun and realized it was past the time when his replacement was supposed to show up. He didn't like it when people were late. He tapped his foot. His tail whipped back and forth. He had promised to help a friend repair one of the tunnels in the burrow that had collapsed. He knew his friend was waiting for him.

Minutes went by and Matt's replacement still hadn't appeared. He paced back and forth until his feet had worn a rut in the dirt. His irritation grew stronger and stronger by the second. Matt was not known for his patience. His parents and aunts and uncles had told him many times that he needed to be more patient, but he just couldn't figure out how to make that happen.

Matt knew he wasn't supposed to leave his guard duty. But as the sun began to dip down, his impatience got the better of him. He got tired of waiting and decided to leave his guard post. Almost all of the meerkats had already returned to the burrow. He figured it wasn't that big a deal. And his friend was waiting for him. And surely the next guard was on his way. Again, he told himself that it was no big deal.

But it was a big deal. He was almost to the entrance hole of the burrow when he heard the squealing. A hungry hyena had snuck into the camp and grabbed a young meerkat. For a few long minutes they couldn't get to the young pup. Thankfully, four of the older meerkats were close by and were able to rescue her.

When Matt found out what happened he was relieved. But he was also crushed. His impatience had almost cost a life.

When his uncle found out he'd left his post before his replacement arrived, he was furious. "What were you thinking? You know that we must have a guard on duty at all times!"

Matt hung his head in shame. "I'm sorry, Uncle. I wasn't thinking clearly. I know there's no excuse, but my replacement was late, and I had made a promise."

"You are correct, Mathlo. There is never any good excuse for leaving your post. I'm afraid you will not be able to guard the clan again. Not until you can prove that you can be patient."

"But how will I do that?" Matt asked.

"I have some ideas, but let me think on it," his uncle said. "We will spend some time together each day doing things that will test your patience. I know you will learn."

"What kind of things will we do?" Matt asked. He had no idea how patience could be tested.

"We will talk about it tomorrow," his uncle replied.

"Why can't you tell me now?" asked Matt.

His uncle sighed. "Your impatience is showing, Mathlo. "Patience means waiting. So go home now. We will talk tomorrow."

After Matt helped his friend repair the burrow wall, he went home and spent the rest of the evening thinking about what had happened. It would take a very long time before anyone would trust him again. His lack of patience had ruined his good name. Learning to wait would take a lot of work, but Matt was determined to become a patient meerkat.

Chapter Three

Morapedi

(One Who Prays)

Morapedi loved to pray. At any given moment, he could be found sitting under a mopane tree with his eyes closed. Everyone knew not to disturb him while he was praying. When Morapedi was praying, he lost all track of time. So, it's probably no big surprise that Morapedi was often late. Late for meals, late for training sessions, late for guard duties, and late for anything else he could possibly be late for.

In fact, it was Morapedi's tardiness that caused his friend, Mathlo, all that trouble. Mathlo still hadn't forgiven him for showing up late for guard duty, but Morapedi kept praying for him. Morapedi prayed for everyone. And he also prayed not to be late to guard duty ever again. He'd been given a very big scolding. So, he opened his eyes and looked at the sun. Oh no, he was late. Again.

He scurried to the top of the guard hill and met Masego. "I'm so sorry. I know I'm late. Can you forgive me? Can you? I hope you can forgive me because forgiveness is very important. I pray about it all the time. So, do you forgive me? Do you?"

Masego sighed. He knew Morapedi prayed a lot. But he also knew that Morapedi talked a lot.

Especially when he was nervous. A regular chatterbox. Masego put his arm around his friend. "I forgive you."

"Ok. Phew. Because I was really worried that you wouldn't forgive me. I'm trying really hard not to be late anymore, but it just keeps happening. I'm not sure how to fix it because when I'm talking to God I have so much to say and I forget about everything else. I 'm really and truly sorry. Really."

"No problem," said Masego. "You're here now. I'm leaving. I will see you tomorrow. Please don't be late. I have something important to do tomorrow afternoon. Keep on the watch!"

Morapedi nodded. "Will do. Thanks."

But despite the warning, the same thing happened the next day. When Morapedi arrived fifteen minutes late, Masego was so frustrated and angry. He wouldn't listen to Masego's apologies. "A late arrival is a rude arrival," he said. "We will talk about this tomorrow."

Morapedi felt a bit nervous. In the past week, he'd been late so many times that several people were really upset with him. Masego was the third person who'd said they needed to have a talk with him about his tardiness. Morapedi closed his eyes to say a quick prayer about it. But he never said quick prayers.

He'd been praying for quite some time when he heard a loud barking signal. His eyes popped open. "Oh no!"

A pack of hyenas appeared on the edge of the mopane forest. Someone else had raised the alarm and now all the meerkats raced to the safety of the burrow. Morapedi knew he was in big trouble. It was his job to sound the alarm and someone else had done it. As he dove down into the nearest hole to the burrow, he braced himself for the lecture he knew would be coming.

But all the meerkats were scurrying around and didn't seem to notice him. Maybe it wasn't such a big deal after all. He found a quiet place and sat down to pray. But no sooner had he closed his eyes than someone cleared his throat nearby.

Morapedi opened his eyes and swallowed a big gulp of fear. It was Mmusi, the clan ruler. Morapedi knew he was in a heap of trouble. He bowed down and gave a quiet chirp greeting.

Mmusi chirped back. "You know why I'm here, don't you, Morapedi?"

His head dropped to his chest. "Yes, Mmusi."

"I've had a lot of complaints about you lately."

"I know, Mmusi." Morapedi wanted to try to explain all the reasons why he'd been late and why he was praying during his guard duty and missed the hyenas. But he realized the best thing he could do at this point was keep his mouth closed and just listen.

Mmusi put a paw on Morapedi's shoulder. "You're a good boy, Morapedi. You're faithful, loyal, and kind. I see you doing many things for others in the clan. You're always ready to help train the young ones. And that's wonderful. But this problem with tardiness is causing real problems."

"I know, Mmusi."

"And this is not a new problem, is it?"

"No, sir."

"Tell me, please, what you've been doing to be on time."

Morapedi had been given a lot of advice in the past year, but no matter how hard he tried, he just didn't seem to be able to get anywhere on time. He thought about some of the things that others had suggested. His auntie had encouraged him to think of the consequences, like ruining his reputation or that others wouldn't see his good qualities because all they noticed was his tardiness. She also told him that it's important to treat others the way you'd like to be treated. She asked if he'd like to have someone show up late every time he was supposed to be relieved from duty. How would he feel if someone did this to him all of the time?

Then there was what his father had told him, "Tardiness is rude and distracting to others. And it can give the impression that you think you're better than others. That their time is not worth as much as yours." Morapedi hated to think that others might believe that about him.

His favorite uncle had sat him down just a month earlier and talked to him about how to set priorities. Morapedi hadn't understood what a priority was, so his uncle explained that it meant making certain things more important than other things.

Morapedi realized that he really hadn't been making being on time a priority. "I guess I haven't really been doing anything, Mmusi. I'm so sorry."

"I appreciate your apology, Morapedi. But I need more than an apology from you. I need you to make me a promise."

"What promise?" he asked.

Mmusi stared straight into his eyes. "I need you to promise me that being on time will be at the top of your list from now on."

Morapedi nodded.

"I'm afraid if things don't change, you will have to be relieved of all your guard duties. So can you promise to be on time?"

Morapedi got quiet. He wasn't sure he could make that promise. He thought about it for a moment. Then he gave his response. "I can promise that I will do my best to be on time. I promise that."

Mmusi smiled. "Ok. I will be keeping an eye on your progress."

After he'd gone, Morapedi closed his eyes and prayed. He prayed that from that day on, he'd be able to be on time. And he prayed the same prayer every day. Again, and Again. And he applied the advice he'd been given. He made it a top priority, and he checked the time more often, and he knew that he would not want someone to treat him that way. And before long, Morapedi was on time. Sometimes he was even early.

Chapter Four

Mothusi (Helper)

Of all the meerkats in the clan, Mothusi was the one everyone went to for help. She loved doing things for others.

Sometimes she'd stay up late into the night taking care of a sick little one. Other times she'd get up super early in the morning to gather food for some of the older meerkats who couldn't get food for themselves. As a consequence, Mothusi was often very, very tired.

On this particular day, Mothusi had both stayed awake late into the night and had also been up super early in the morning. She thought she would have time to take a nap before her guard duty in the afternoon, but then her cousin asked her if she could babysit her newborn triplets for a few hours after lunch. She loved taking care of newborn babies, so she couldn't say no, even though she was very, very tired.

Normally, Mothusi was the most reliable of all the meerkats in the clan. If she said she was going to be somewhere at a certain time, others could count on her. She'd be there. She knew that some had been late for their guard duties and it had caused all kinds of trouble, so she made sure that she arrived at her guard post on the hill a little early.

The guard on duty was very grateful. "Thanks for coming early. I'm dying of hunger." He shook her paw and scurried off to find something to eat.

Mothusi settled into her post, eyes wide open. She turned slowly in each direction, scanning the skies and the delta for any signs of dangerous animals. But after a little while, her eyelids started to feel very heavy. And as time went on, they got heavier and heavier. She walked in circles to try to keep herself awake. But no matter how hard she tried, her eyelids were just too heavy. She couldn't keep them from falling over her eyes.

Every few seconds she would jerk herself awake. Falling asleep on guard duty was a big no no. She should have chirped for someone to come and take over her duty, but Mothusi wanted to be reliable and responsible. She wanted to fulfill her duty. So, she did everything she could to stay awake. But she still failed.

A voice shouted in her ear. "Mothusi! Get up!"

She opened her eyes to six angry faces staring down at her. It took her a few seconds to come fully awake and remember where she was. Her heart sunk into her stomach. She jumped to her feet. "Did something happen? Did anyone get hurt?"

"Everyone is safe. But we're relieving you of your guard duties. You will be on suspension for the next month."

Mothusi blinked back her tears. She'd let everyone down. She couldn't be trusted anymore. Her heart ached as she crept back to the burrow hole and made her way to her room. She curled up on her bed and cried herself to sleep.

Someone stood beside her with a paw on her shoulder. The voice that spoke sounded gentle and kind. "Mothusi, Mothusi, wake up."

She opened her eyes and looked into her mother's smiling eyes. "Is it morning?"

Her mother shook her head. "It's dinner time. Are you hungry?"

Mothusi shook her head.

"What's wrong, little one? It's not like you to sleep all afternoon. Did something happen?"

Mothusi started to cry again. In between sniffles she explained to her mother what had happened. "I feel like such a terrible failure. Will anyone ever trust me again?"

Her mother sat down beside her and smoothed the fur on Mothusi's head. "Everyone makes mistakes, little one."

"Yes," Mothusi replied. "But my mistake could have cost lives. Someone could have died because I fell asleep on my guard duty."

"True. But they didn't. You've learned a valuable lesson, but thankfully not the hard way. So tell me what you've learned from what happened today?"

"I learned that you should never, never, never fall asleep on a guard duty."

Mothusi's mother nodded. "But sometimes we have to dig a little deeper to find lessons that can lead us to solutions. Can you tell me why you fell asleep in the first place?"

Mothusi cocked her head. "Because I was tired."

"Yes, little one. But why were you so tired?"

Mothusi told her mom about staying up late to help a sick one and how she helped gather food and babysit.

"You are such a giving person, Mothusi. You are a great helper to so many in the clan. But you need to be careful to take care of yourself, too. If you want to be reliable, you need to make sure you always get enough rest."

Mothusi sighed "You're right, mother. I should have come home and taken a nap instead of babysitting the triplets."

"This is true," her mother said. "Someone else could have done the babysitting. But I think there may be something else you need to learn from this experience."

Mothusi waited for her mother to continue.

"You're a great helper, Mothusi, but I think you need to learn to ask for some help of your own sometimes."

"Help with what?" Mothusi asked.

"Well," her mother said. "When you started to feel very sleepy during your guard duty, what could you have done?"

Mothusi thought about it for a bit. "I could have tried harder to stay awake."

"Or you could have asked for help. Someone would have come and relieved you."

"I didn't think about that," Mothusi admitted. "I guess I'm so used to helping others, I never think about asking for help."

"That's exactly the point, little one," her mother said. "Now come eat dinner."

She got up and joined her family for the evening meal. They enjoyed a variety of insects and mushrooms. When Mothusi came back to her room she thought a lot about the things her mother had said. She did have a hard time asking for help. It would be difficult, but she would do her best to ask for help the next time she had a problem. Being fully rested is very important if you want to do a good job.

Chapter Five

Mokgosi

(Loud Cry for Help)

Mokgosi liked to make everyone laugh. She also liked to play practical jokes on the clan. Sometimes her pranks went too far. Like when she was a young pup, she slipped out early one morning and covered all the burrow exits with branches and thick savanna grass. When everyone woke up, there was no light in the burrow and no one could find the exits. Mokgosi got in big trouble for that one. She was grounded for a month.

During her guard duty training, Mokgosi played a few tricks. Because of this, the clan elders decided to wait a few more years before allowing her the privilege of being a guard. Mokgosi really, really, really wanted to be a guard. So she begged and begged and begged to be given a chance. Finally, the day came when they decided to give her guard duties. But before the clan elders approved her, they sat her down for a very serious talk.

"Guard duty is very important. It is not an occasion for fun and games. If we give you a chance, you will have to prove that you can be very responsible. If you play around, even just once, we will take this privilege away from you forever. Do you understand?"

Mokgosi nodded her head up and down with wild enthusiasm. "I promise I will be very serious. Very responsible. I will. I will. I will."

So, they gave her a chance. And for several months she had been proving to be very responsible. Some considered her the best girl guard in the clan. Mokgosi felt very happy and proud of that. And although she still made people laugh every day, she was being very careful to not play any practical jokes on anyone. But that didn't mean she didn't think about playing them.

Sometimes Mokgosi had the urge to bark a false alarm, just to watch everyone scramble underground to the burrows. But Mokgosi had heard stories about animals crying out danger when there was no danger. And then when there really was a danger, no one believed them. Mokgosi didn't want that to happen to her. Her name meant "loud cry for help" and she wanted to make sure if she barked out an alarm that everyone believed her. Meerkat lives were on the line. Unfortunately, some of Mokgosi's young pup friends didn't understand this.

Most of the young pups in the clan loved to hang out with Mokgosi. She was funny and bubbly and made them laugh a lot. They loved her practical jokes. They wanted to be just like her. So while Mokgosi guarded the clan, a group of young ones met together under the biggest Acacia tree and planned a great big practical joke to play on Mokgosi.

"It has to be something that will really surprise her."

"Yeah. Something wild and crazy."

"Something that will make her laugh really hard."

When the young pups had decided on the best possible prank to pull on Mokgosi, they quietly practiced and practiced and practiced some more. When they thought they were finally ready, they hurried back toward the burrow to put their plan into action. They couldn't stop giggling with excitement. But as they skipped past Mokgosi at her guard post, they all shushed each other.

Mokgosi noticed their peculiar behavior. "What are you pups up to today?"

The young meerkats smirked and just kept walking. Mokgosi's whiskers twitched and she cocked her head to one side. Something was definitely going on with that group. And she would find out soon enough.

The afternoon had been quiet. No danger from the blue sky above. No danger from the sandy delta below. Mokgosi actually preferred a little excitement, but she felt happy that all the meerkats were safe and could go about their business without being interrupted. She glanced at the sun. Fifteen minutes until her shift was over. Her tummy growled. She hoped her replacement would show up soon. She hadn't eaten anything since breakfast and that was ages ago. But Mokgosi quickly forgot about her stomach.

All of a sudden, alarms sounded from all around her—chirrups, trills, growls, and barks. Mokgosi searched the sky and earth and couldn't see any sign of danger. Had she missed something?

The entire clan raced around in wild chaos, desperate to get underground. Meerkats bumped into each other and toppled over. Others tripped and fell. Still, others tripped over eachother and went down in a cloud of dust. Mokgosi had never seen anything like it. She scanned the area from left to right and up and down and still couldn't see any sign of danger. Then she caught sight of something odd at the edge of the water. The young pups were standing in a circle, doubled over in laughter.

It didn't take Mokgosi long to figure out what had happened. And she knew that soon there would be big trouble. She just hoped that the trouble wouldn't come to her door. Would the clan elders hold her responsible for a trick played on her by a group of younger meerkats? She wouldn't have long to wait to find out. Three clan elders were headed straight for her. And they were not smiling.

"Mokgosi!" One of them yelled as they raced up the hill. "How could you?"

She waited until they got close and caught their breath before she tried to explain. She turned to point to the group of naughty young ones, but they had disappeared. Of course. How was she going to prove that she hadn't put them up to it?

One way or another, Mokgosi knew she'd be blamed for what happened, so she figured she should just apologize and accept her punishment. "As soon as my replacement arrives, I will leave this guard post for good," she said in a low, sad voice.

The clan elders frowned and nodded. "You knew the consequences."

When she got home, Mokgosi went straight to her room and thought about what had happened. She realized that in some ways it was her fault. She had set a bad example for the young ones. They didn't think about the harm that could come from practical jokes. And it wasn't a big surprise that the pups had wanted to imitate her. A tap on the door startled her out of her thoughts. It was her father.

"Can you come out. The clan elders want to have a talk with you."

Mokgosi let out a big sigh and dragged herself into the family's large den. The clan elders smiled and greeted her. "We have good news for you. Mokgosi."

Her eyes widened. "Good news?"

"Yes. We've decided not to remove you from your guard duties."

Mokgosi sighed in relief. "Thank you so much. But why did you change your minds?"

They explained to her that the young pups had come and confessed to them. "We now know that you didn't put them up to it. Not directly anyway."

"Right." Mokgosi shook their paws. "Thanks for giving me another chance."

The clan elders left and Mokgosi skipped back to her room in happiness. As she curled up to go to sleep, she made a decision. She would still make people laugh, but she would no longer play practical jokes that could cause trouble, danger, or harm to others.

Chapter Six

Malebogo (Thanks)

Malebogo really loved to eat and was very grateful to anyone who would bring her food. Especially when she was on guard duty. But most of the meerkats knew that guards weren't supposed to eat while they were keeping watch. Eating too much can be distracting and make one sleepy. Guards needed to be very careful to stay alert and not to fall asleep on their watch. So Malebogo did her best to forget about food while she guarded the clan. But not eating was very, very, very hard for her.

Within the first five minutes of taking over the duty, Malebogo heard a <u>trilling</u> scream. She recognized the call. A chill ran down her spine. One of the meerkats had encountered a Cape Cobra. These large snakes were one of the clan's biggest enemies. One bite from one of those large poisonous snakes could mean instant death for a meerkat.

As Malebogo watched from a distance, the entire clan gathered for the fight. Malebogo wanted to join them in the battle, but she knew she couldn't leave her post. Instead she had to keep her eyes open for any other dangers that might come from sky or land. But she could still watch what was happening with the fight.

A dozen meerkats circled around the large beige cobra. The hood around its neck flared out as it raised itself off the ground and rose a foot in the air. The meerkats stood on their hind legs and showed the cobra their sharp teeth. The cobra hissed and lunged at the meerkats. They dodged and darted back and forth, attacking the cobra from all sides. The cobra struck out at them again and again. But the meerkats were quick on their feet and were able to avoid the cobra strikes. After a little while, the cobra gave up and slithered off out of the colony and into the forest.

Malebogo let out a huge sigh of relief and gave her full attention to keeping the clan safe. But she had a hard time concentrating. Her stomach growled and rumbled. It had been several hours since she'd last eaten and her tummy ached with emptiness. She searched the ground around her for insects. A couple millipedes would satisfy her just fine. But there was not one single thing to eat on the hill, not even one little bug. So Malebogo tried to forget about her hunger and focus on her job.

But her stomach kept talking and growling. And talking and growling. And talking and growling. She was so hungry.

Several young meerkats walked close by and Malebogo whistled to get their attention. But when she asked them to go fetch her a little snack, they shook their heads. "Guards aren't supposed to eat while they're working." And they continued on their way.

Malebogo groaned. Did all the meerkats in the clan know about that rule? What she needed to find was a rebel meerkat. Someone who didn't care about breaking the rules. She needed a little something to eat or she wouldn't be able to concentrate. And she knew just the meerkat to help her—Kenosi. His name meant "I am alone" and Kenosi really was a loner. He did his own thing. And he wasn't afraid of getting in trouble.

So Malebogo motioned at one of the young meerkats who was playing nearby. "Could you please go find Kenosi and tell him I want to talk with him?"

"What do you need from Kenosi?" the young meerkat asked with suspicion. "What do you want to talk to him about?"

Malebogo put her hands on her hips and made her stern guard face. "Just go get him and stop asking questions."

"Yes, Ma'am." The young meerkat scurried off in a hurry.

While she waited, Malebogo paced back and forth from one end of the hill to the other. The pain of emptiness in her stomach got bigger and bigger. She scanned the delta in all directions in search of Kenosi. What was taking him so long?

If felt like forever before she finally spotted a small dot heading toward the guard hill. She looked closer and sighed in relief when she recognized the clan rebel. As was his custom, Kenosi moved slow like a three-toed sloth. Even when there was danger. He just didn't seem to care about getting anywhere in a hurry. She hoped he would be in a happy mood. Kenosi was often grumpy. If he was grouchy, he might not be willing to fetch food for her.

When Kenosi finally arrived on the hill, he frowned at Malebogo. "I hope this is something important."

Malebogo cringed. He most definitely seemed grouchy. She knew she needed to choose her words carefully, so she took a minute to think before answering. She needed to poke at his rebellious side. "You know about the silly no food on guard duty rule, right?"

Kenosi snorted. "Just one of many silly rules."

Malebogo smiled. "So how would you feel about breaking that rule for me. I'm starving!"

"Sure," said Kenosi. "What do you want?"

"A couple of plump lizards would be just perfect."

Kenosi nodded. "I'll see what I can find."

Malebogo wanted to tell him to make it quick, but she knew better. Saying that would just make him go slower. So, she kept her mouth shut.

Much to her surprise, Kenosi returned in less than ten minutes. Each of his paws held a big, fat lizard. He handed them over to Malebogo who immediately gulped them down. "Thanks, Kenosi. I owe you one."

"Actually," he said. "You owe me a lot more than one. You owe me a thousand."

Malebogo shook her head. "I don't understand. What do you mean by that?"

Kenosi frowned. "The price. For the lizards. You didn't think I would come all this way and then go hunt food for you for free, did you?"

Malebogo hadn't thought about being charged. She thought he would just do her the favor. "I'd be happy to pay you, but you're kidding about the thousand thing, right?"

He pointed to his serious face. "Do I look like I'm kidding?"

A bad feeling washed over Malebogo. "How come you didn't tell me about the cost before you got the lizards for me?"

"You didn't ask," he said.

"Well I'm not paying you a thousand. A thousand what, anyway?"

"A thousand lizards. And yes. You will pay me."

Malebogo laughed. "Yeah? And if I don't. What will you do to me?"

Kenosi shrugged. "I will tell the clan elders that you ate on the job. And you will no longer have guard privileges."

"You wouldn't do that, would you?"

Kenosi smirked. "I would."

"Where am I supposed to get a thousand lizards?" asked Malebogo.

"How about I strike a deal with you," said Kenosi. "You give me two a day for the next year and we'll call it even."

Malebogo shook her head. "You can't be serious."

"Hey, that's a huge discount. You're saving over 250." Kenosi put out his paw for her to shake. "Is it a deal?"

Malebogo thought about it. She really had no choice. So, she shook his hand. "Deal."

"You can bring them to me every morning. I'll be waiting by the big Acacia tree."

Malebogo nodded. As Kenosi walked away she kicked at the dirt. How could she have been so dumb? She let her stomach get the best of her. And she knew better than to trust a rebel. A rule breaker. And now she would have to spend a year fetching lizards for him every morning? From that day on, she made sure she planned ahead and ate plenty of food before she started her guard duty. She would do the right thing and not break the rules from here on out. She learned her lesson. She also decided that she should come clean and tell the truth to the clan elders. She didn't want this secret hanging over her head for a whole year. If she lost her guard privileges, then so be it. She had to take responsibility for her actions. It was the right thing to do.

Will You Help Us Out?

Would you please consider leaving reviews online for our books because they help so much? They don't have to be long and will only take a minute. It would mean a lot and help us get the word out, to other children, as well. Thank you so much! We are extremely grateful.

AFTERWORD

Thanks again for picking up this book! You are participating in making our world a better place to live and grow. When children learn that they will always get back what they give, they will start to navigate their lives in incredible ways. When you give a smile, and make someone's heart feel lighter and happier, you can be sure that you will receive something in the near future that will make your heart happier as well. When you do something kind for someone, you can be sure that someone will do something kind for you in the coming days ahead. It's truly amazing how it works! Have fun with it and enjoy!

For more of our *Karma for Kids Books* please visit us at:

www.findyourwaypublishing.com

Find Norma MacDonald books online at Amazon.com.

Can Camels Dance? Short Stories, Fuzzy Animals, and Life Lessons

Arctic Adventures: Short Stories, Fuzzy Animals, and Life Lessons

Kyle Kitten and Friends: Short Stories, Fuzzy Animals, and Life Lessons

The Panda Family Relies on Each Other: Short Stories, Fuzzy Animals, and Life Lessons

Matt the African Meerkat and Friends: Short Stories, Fuzzy Animals, and Life Lessons

The Many Adventures of Peppy the Emperor Penguin: Short Stories, Fuzzy Animals, and Life Lessons

Kimmie Koala and Friends: Short Stories, Fuzzy Animals, and Life Lessons

Cranky Crocodile Saves the Day: Short Stories, Fuzzy Animals, and Life Lessons

Lucy Llama and Friends: Short Stories, Fuzzy Animals, and Life Lessons

Ethan the Eagle and Friends; Short Stories, Fuzzy Animals, and Life Lessons

Billy Brown Bear and Friends; Short Stories, Fuzzy Animals, and Life Lessons

Humble Heron and Friends; Short Stories, Fuzzy Animals, and Life Lessons

Peter Penguin and Friends; Short Stories, Fuzzy Animals, and Life Lessons

Alexei the Siberian Tiger and Friends at the Circus: Short Stories, Fuzzy Animals, and Life Lessons

Pedro the Amazon Rainforest Parrot and Friends: Short Stories, Fuzzy Animals, and Life Lessons

Other books that we recommend to help children learn important life lessons:

Guaranteed Success for Kindergarten; 50 Easy Things You Can Do Today! by Marrae Kimball

Guaranteed Success for Grade School; 50 Easy Things You Can Do Today! by Marrae Kimball

The Secret Combination to Middle School: Real Advice from Real Kids, Ideas for Success, and Much More! by Marrae Kimball

High School Success: How to Create Your Own Path, Beat Anxiety & Depression, Master Your Goals & Dreams
by Marrae Kimball

Again, thank you for reading and sharing this book! YOU are making the world a better place. Would you please consider leaving a short review for our books, online, because they help us spread the message! Children deserve the very best that life has to offer. Reviews don't have to be long, a few sentences will do, and they help more than you know! Thank you!

All children deserve a chance at a successful and happy life.

If you have ideas for stories, please feel free to share and send them to:

Melissa Eshleman
Find Your Way Publishing, Inc.
PO Box 667
Norway, ME 04268
Melissa@findyourwaypublishing.com

www.findyourwaypublishing.com

Thank you!

Disclaimer

The purpose of this book is for entertainment purposes only. This book is designed to provide information and motivation to our readers. The content of each story is the sole expression and opinion of its author, and not necessarily that of the publisher. Names, characters, businesses, places, and incidents are either the products of the authors' imaginations or used in a fictitious manner. Any resemblance to actual persons, living or dead, businesses, companies, events, locales, or actual events is entirely coincidental. This book is not intended nor is it implied to be a substitute for professional medical advice, and any medical advice and any medical information contained in this book is not intended to be diagnostic or treatment in any way. The author and publisher are not engaged in rendering medical, psychological, legal, or any other professional services. If medical, psychological or other expert assistance is required, please talk to your physician and locate the services of a competent professional. The author and publisher shall have neither liability nor responsibility to any person or entity with respect to any loss or damage caused, or alleged to have been caused, directly or indirectly, by the information contained in this book. Neither the publisher nor the individual author(s) shall be liable for any physical, psychological, emotional, financial, or commercial damages, including, but not limited to, special, incidental, consequential or other damages. If you do not wish to be bound by the above, you may return this book along with a copy of the receipt to the publisher for a full refund.

www.ingramcontent.com/pod-product-compliance
Lightning Source LLC
Chambersburg PA
CBHW070807120626
46557CB00002B/740